OWL OR PUSSYCAT?

www.davidficklingbooks.com

with thanks to Edward Lear

OWL OR PUSSYCAT?
is a DAVID FICKLING BOOK
First published in hardback in Great Britain in 2020 by
David Fickling Books,
31 Beaumont Street,
Oxford, OX1 2NP

This edition published in 2022

978-1-78845-073-7

www.davidficklingbooks.com

Text © Michael Morpurgo, 2020
Illustrations © Polly Dunbar, 2020

1 3 5 7 9 10 8 6 4 2

WARNING: THIS BOOK WILL MELT YOUR HEART

Papers used by David Fickling Books are from well-managed forests and other responsible sources.

MIX
Paper from
responsible sources
FSC® C104723
FSC
www.fsc.org

DAVID FICKLING BOOKS Reg. No. 8340307
A CIP catalogue record for this book is available from the British Library.
Printed and bound in China by Toppan Leefung

Edited by Alice Corrie
Designed by Ness Wood

MICHAEL MORPURGO

Presents

OWL OR PUSSYCAT?

With set design by

POLLY DUNBAR

David Fickling Books

*A story written for the children of St Cuthbert with St. Matthias,
my very first school, and quite a lot of it is true.*

Honest.

Michael Morpurgo, 2020

Once upon a time, a long, long time ago, when I was a little boy, I went to a school called St Cuthbert's on the Warwick Road. We lived not far away in a place called Philbeach Gardens, number 44, I think it was. I did lots of things in that school for the first time.

I learnt to read my first book,

write my first words,

add up my first numbers.

But the day I remember best, was the day I acted in my first play.

It was a play called *The Owl and the Pussycat*. Our teacher made us all learn the poem, by Edward Lear. You would love it! And then one by one we all had to stand up and recite it. It begins:

The Owl and the Pussy-cat went to sea
In a beautiful pea-green boat:
They took some honey and plenty of money,
Wrapped up in a five-pound note . . .

I loved the rhythm of it and the fun of it, and the pictures it made in my mind. At home my mum had read it to me often. So when it was my turn to stand up and recite the poem to the class, I did it without a mistake, and felt very pleased with myself. And my teacher said:

"Very good, Michael. Because you did that so well, *you* will play Owl in our school play this Christmas."

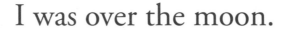

I was over the moon.

My mother was over the moon.

I had the starring part in the school Christmas play, which we always had in the school hall upstairs, and all the parents and all the teachers would be there, and every child in the school.

The school hall was the biggest and grandest room I had ever been in, with a
polished parquet wood floor that we always sat on for assemblies. I loved the
patterns in that floor.

Rehearsals were great.
There were songs and dances.

Everyone had a part,
not just me.

But *I* had the **biggest** part.

I was Owl.

I didn't just say 'hello' to
people now, or 'good morning', I said . . .

. . . Too —

Wit-too-woooooo

I liked being Owl all day long.

I had a wonderful Owl costume made for me, covered in Owl feathers.

I had Owl ears, Owl beak, Owl claws.

I was Owl all over!

Best of all, though,
the girl who was chosen
to play Pussycat
was my best friend . . .

. . . Belinda.

And in the play I had to sing her a song on my guitar.

They made me a pretend guitar, and I had
to pretend to play on it, while the teacher
played on the piano as I sang the song.

It was the only bit of the play
I did not like, because
it was a love song.

And I loved Belinda.

I had never told her that.
                    Of course not.

I was six years old
                    and I was too shy.

She was another first.

The first girl I ever loved.

Somehow I found it hard
to pretend to play the guitar,
to remember the words *and* the
notes of my song, *and* to look
at Belinda at the same time, as the
teacher said I should.

And here's why . . .

Belinda was sitting opposite me in the beautiful pea-green boat, dressed in her bright-white furry cat costume, with a long bushy tail. And she had whiskers too. And all the time *I* was singing, the teacher told her to miaow loudly all the way through, which made everyone laugh.

Except me, because the truth was that I meant every single word of the love song I was singing to her, and it wasn't a laughing matter. And she wasn't even listening to me. She was too busy miaowing and getting laughs.

So I *never* looked forward to singing her my song.

And there was something else that was bothering me too.

Belinda was really good at being Pussycat. So good that all through rehearsals it was obvious *she* was becoming the star of the show.

miaOW

Her costume was gorgeous.

She was more catlike than any cat I ever saw.

And worst of all she got *all* the laughs!

No one seemed that interested in poor old Owl.

I was getting *really* fed up.
So fed up, in fact, that I was
beginning to think I wasn't
that keen on Belinda after all.

The Show was on!

It was all going so well. They were clapping every song, every dance.

And I hadn't forgotten any lines.

The great day came. On the afternoon of the play, on the last day of term before Christmas, there was great excitement in the school hall. The decorations were up. Paper chains everywhere. A Christmas tree was in the corner. Between us, up on the stage, and the audience, there was a curtain.

The buzz on the other side of that curtain was
the most exciting sound I had ever heard.
My mum was out there, my aunties and
my grandmother too. It sounded like
half of London was there as well.

Suddenly

the curtain

was opened . . .

Then it came to the moment
when I picked up the guitar from
the bottom of the pea-green boat
and began to play . . .

. . . Except I didn't. I couldn't.

My mind, frozen.

My voice, frozen.

My heart, frozen.

The teacher played the introduction to my song again. There was a deeply worried look on her face. She was mouthing at me, like a frightened goldfish.

She was trying to help me but it was no good.

Belinda was looking at me out of her wide pussycat eyes.
She also knew I had forgotten my words and was
trying to mouth something to help me too.

I felt the tears coming.

And then a miracle happened . . .

Suddenly Belinda leaned forward,
took the guitar off me and began
to sing my song, word perfect.
Better than I had ever done it.

My tears stopped.

Belinda had saved my life!

And do you
know what I did?

I started to miaow, just as *she* had done in rehearsals.

There was a great paper moon hanging over the stage.

I miaowed to that moon,

I caterwauled to that moon:

no one had ever serenaded a moon better.

Miaow Miaoow Miaooooo

And the more
the audience
laughed,
the **louder** and
the **better** I did it.

When we had finished, they gave us both a standing ovation. And I could see my mum was crying with laughter and pride out there.

It was the best moment of my life.

Afterwards, as we walked home together through the park,
Belinda said nothing about me forgetting my words.

She just said: "We was good. You miaow really well."

And I said: "You sing really well."

"I know," she said. "See you."

She meant, "Love you."

Of course I knew that.

So I said "See you" too.

The Owl and the Pussy-Cat

By Edward Lear

The Owl and the Pussy-Cat went to sea
In a beautiful pea-green boat:
They took some honey and plenty of money
Wrapped up in a five-pound note.
The Owl looked up to the stars above,
And sang to a small guitar,
"O lovely Pussy! O Pussy, my love,
What a beautiful Pussy you are,
You are!
You are!
What a beautiful Pussy you are!"

Pussy said to the Owl, "You elegant fowl,
How charmingly sweet you sing!
Oh! Let us be married, too long we have tarried.
But what shall we do for a ring?" . . .

They sailed away, for a year and a day,
… to the land where the Bong-Tree grows;
And there in a wood a Piggy-Wig stood,
With a ring at the end of his nose,
His nose,
His nose,
With a ring at the end of his nose.

"Dear Pig, are you willing to sell for one shilling
Your ring?" said the Piggy, "I will."
So they took it away, and were married next day
By the Turkey who lives on the hill.

They dined on mince and slices of quince,
Which they ate with a runcible spoon;
And hand in hand, on the edge of the sand,
They danced by the light of the moon,
                                        The moon,
                                                    The moon,
They danced by the light of the moon.

Michael Morpurgo

is the best-selling author of more than a hundred children's books, including *Private Peaceful* and *War Horse*, which became a smash-hit theatre play and a film. Michael and his wife Clare also run Farms for City Children, a charity they founded which gives children and teachers from urban primary schools the chance to live and work in the countryside for a week.

www.michaelmorpurgo.com

Polly Dunbar

is the creator of many much loved books for children, including the best-selling and award-winning *Penguin* and *Tilly and Friends*, which became a popular television series. She is also co-founder of Long Nose Puppets, an award-winning theatre company that has made successful adaptations of *Shoe Baby, Fly Away Katie, Penguin* and *Arthur's Dream Boat*.

www.pollydunbar.com